McShayne's Dragon

McShayne Bloodline #1

Nicole Dennis

Blurb:

Betrayed, Morric McShayne, a bloodline elemental witch, wakes during a lightning storm, bound to a post—the latest sacrifice to appease a dragon. He swears to survive as the last McShayne and there is no dragon until a powerful claw plucks him away from the precipice.

With every equinox, the dragon's keeper, Xavier, pushes back the loneliness. The keeper holds a secret until magic flares. This sacrifice is different.

They battle desire and duty. When a single kiss changes everything, can the Fae help them answer more secrets and a legend's promise? Do they fight against Fate's choice?

All rights reserved

This literary work may not be reproduced or transmitted in any form or by any means, including electronic or photographic reproduction, in whole or in part, without express written permission. This book cannot be copied in any format, sold, or otherwise transferred from your computer to another through upload to a file sharing peer-to-peer program, for free or for a fee. Such action is illegal and in violation of Copyright Law.

NO AI/NO BOT. We do not consent to any Artificial Intelligence (AI), generative AI, large language model, machine learning, chatbot, or other automated analysis, generative process, or replication program to reproduce, mimic, remix, summarize, or otherwise replicate any part of this creative work, via any means: print, graphic, sculpture, multimedia, audio, or other medium. We support the right of humans to control their artistic works.

McShayne's Dragon is a work of fiction. Names, characters, places, and incidents are the products of the author's imagination or are used fictitiously. Any resemblance to actual events, locales, or persons, living or dead, is entirely coincidental.

All rights reserved, including the right of reproduction in whole or in part in any form. For permission requests and all other inquiries, contact: nicoledennis.author@gmail.com

Second Ebook Publication & Copyright © November 2021 by FatCat Books Ink

Cover Art and Edited by Kris Jacen

Cover content is for illustrative purposes only and any person depicted on the cover is a model.

https://www.krisjacen.com/three-hearts

Chapter One

There had to be an ironic explanation for this entire situation. It couldn't possibly be reality, but this felt more than a simple dream, even the nastiest nightmare.

Morric McShayne blinked open his crusty eyelids. His vision blurred and darkened. His head ached and felt heavy. He didn't remember taking one of his sleeping potions to help get past one of the many sleepless nights. Thanks to that blasted dream and those eyes haunting him. Those brilliant emerald eyes. He didn't know who those eyes belonged too. A rich tenor tone with a lilting accent whispered *mate* to him. The voice went with those eyes.

Only he didn't dream those eyes tonight. This wasn't a dream. This wasn't even a regular sleep. This was something else.

Morric wiggled his jaw. A harsh flare of pain spread across one cheekbone. He winced against it, then groaned and mumbled under his breath.

Drugged and punched. What in the name of the Crone did I do this time? Give someone the wrong tea?

No, someone gave him the wrong tea. At the town meeting last night.

Morric remembered performing the vernal equinox dance within his protective circle to spread nature's energy into the land. He'd reenergized the forest and land after the long winter's sleep and prepared it to accept and grow the new seed. While he danced, he pulled down the energy and light from the full moon to replenish the earth. The gifts of the three Blessed Ladies joined him to bring life back. Of course, he did all this sky-clad, as was his custom with all his equinox dances. Only when he finished did he feel someone's gaze upon him. Someone invaded his sanctuary. Dark hateful energy came with the obtrusive gaze and broke harsh against the welcoming warm energy and light created by the dance.

After pulling on his robes, he returned to his snug cabin. Dressing, he groomed himself in proper "town" attire. He left his beloved forest to head into town for the dreaded meeting. He rarely went into the small town, but it was one of those mandatory town-hall meetings that happen every season. If he didn't go, the town would try to pass some new law to make all his work illegal or take away his lands and plow through the forest to make way for some new farming land. They tried it exactly once when he didn't go to a meeting and he made sure either option would never pass. No one tried to propose the law again, but he made enemies with his vehement determination to protect his life and the forest.

Something happened at last night's meeting.

The memories were fuzzy, but Morric remembered accepting the cup from Lady Jackson. That was the only time he didn't keep track of where his cup of tea came from. After that, the night became a blank.

Wake up, Morric! Figure out what's going on. You're not home. Trouble. This all means trouble. In the name of the Crone, wake up!

Bright light flashed. The deep rumble of thunder grew into a raucous roar. The sound of it vibrated the very Earth. Cold droplets continued to splash across his skin. His russet brown hair draped past his shoulders; thick wet strands flopped across his face. Clothing hung against his body, saturated and clinging to his chilled skin. His shoulders ached. When he tried to pull them down, he couldn't budge his arms.

Wait. Earth? Rain? Lightning? What in the name of sweet Maiden is happening?

Morric forced himself to focus when he opened his eyes. This time he made sure they stayed open. He needed to figure out what was happening to him. His life, his forest, and his magic depended on staying awake and focused.

Sometime during the night, a fierce storm descended upon their small section of earth. Located at the very edge of the forested land, against the vast ocean, Morric knew thunderstorms could become vicious with all the moisture surrounding them. Even tucked in his cozy thatched cottage protected by powerful ancient oaks, Morric didn't dare venture outside into one of these storms. This wasn't the welcoming kind of rain to soak the ground with life-giving water. This storm could become a life-taker.

Now, somehow, he stood in the vast open. He was literally surrounded by the storm's wrath.

"Sweet Maiden, this isn't good."

Stating the obvious didn't help his predicament look any better.

Morric tilted his head and followed his arms up into the night. Wide iron cuffs secured around his wrists, locked tight, and connected to long heavy chains. He wiggled his fingers and hands, but couldn't spread them further to find a way to escape. The iron in his cuffs caused his energy to spark and flutter.

An elemental witch with some Fae heritage, Morric hated the feel of iron on his skin. Luckily, the iron wouldn't burn his skin like his ancestors, but it made him uncomfortable. It created a prickly buzzing type of feeling that wouldn't dissipate. His magic and energy were fuzzy behind the iron shield, almost lost to him. Thanks to the aching pull against his joints, he knew the stretch of his arms went almost too far and far too long.

"I'm not trussed up here like a turkey to be comfortable."

He studied how someone secured the chains to the iron ring connected to a post. The post had been planted deep into the rocky ground.

Oh, sweet Maiden, this can't be real.

Morric realized exactly where he was.

The sacrifice precipice.

A glance down gave him the final answer. The pure white robe of a sacrifice with a simple shirt and pants underneath. His feet bare on the cold ground. The fabric almost translucent from the torrential downpour.

Morric screamed his outrage to the night. He tugged his wrists against the cuffs, rattled the chains against the pole, and only caused more tugging on his shoulders. It was pointless to continue screaming. It did nothing to fix the situation, but he got it off his chest.

Sacrifices? Really. The idea of them was so outrageous and outdated. The nature and beliefs rooted strong in the small town that grew next to his forest over the generations of his family.

For years, the townspeople believed a dragon lived in the northern mountains. They insisted how the dragon controlled the weather and the destiny of the growing and harvest seasons. Without the dragon's approval, the town wouldn't have a successful season and could potentially starve during the endless winters. For this reason, the townspeople decreed they would offer a sacrifice to appease the dragon. A human sacrifice. Since that decree, Morric lost track of how many young people were lost to this archaic belief system.

"Superstitious fools. Dragons are extinct. Everyone knows this fact. No one has seen a dragon in a generation."

Personally, Morric considered the whole dragon idea impossible. As a male bloodline witch, he dealt with superstitions and the unusual throughout his life. The townspeople considered his work unnatural, his witchcraft abilities influenced by demons. Nothing could be further from the truth. Everything he worked with came from nature. He used what nature provided in a different fashion to create the potions, teas, medicines and other items. Items the townspeople used every single day. Some of them even came to him to help cure their various ailments or with pleas to help further their desires and wishes, but would immediately flip when asked to accuse him of horrible deeds and black witchcraft.

What happened this time to make them decide I would be the sacrifice?

He tried to think about the last few people who requested his help, but it wasn't anything out of the ordinary. The usual teas to help with arthritis or breathing issues. A box of his beeswax candles. None of that could cause an uproar.

It had to be the person lurking in the forest, observing his lunar dance.

Another bright crack of lightning pierced the sky. The multi-forked slash illuminated the darkness.

Morric took advantage to lower his gaze. Close enough to the edge, he followed the long drop down the cliffs. It was well over a mile below to the frothy water. His stomach turned. He felt woozy. He never did well around heights.

Not that he had the particular problem of an accidental tumble this evening. Oh no, his was a far more desperate situation.

Another heated curse escaped him at the feat the townspeople accomplished. Somehow, he'd become their latest sacrifice. Like all the previous sacrifices, he wouldn't return to his beloved cottage, garden and protective circle. If he didn't return, the land would die. The town's crops wouldn't grow as numerous or strong. He connected to the earth and sky and repaired the damage done by the town. Now his beloved forest would die.

No one knew exactly what happened to the sacrifice. Everyone feared the dragon wouldn't appear if someone stayed to guard or watch the sacrifice through the night. No, they all walked away, leaving the sacrifice to their eventual death. If it came to that.

Morric swore they didn't disappear by a dragon. Perhaps someone from another town learned about the sacrificial offerings and returned to help them.

"For all their foolish superstitious fears, I can't believe they would truss me up here." Morric banged the back of his head against the pole. "I didn't think those old farts had the balls. Impressive, but beloved Triple Goddess—" He paused to gaze up at the storming sky, eyes closing when the rain droplets stung his face. "This isn't how I want my days to end. Beloved Triple Goddess, protect me, guide me, and reveal to me how to leave this path."

High rolling waves broke against the series of granite breakers. The spray crashed against the dangerous granite and shale cliffs. The water created a mist around the precipice, altering the edge to make it harder to find. He felt the additional spray against his chilled skin, the taste of the salt against his lips.

His knees shook with weakness, only the chains kept him upright.

"Enough, I'm stronger than this. I can get free."

Morric needed to regain lost energy before he could figure out a way to get free. Nature provided more than enough tonight. He tossed a drenched russet lock away from his eye, but it didn't quite work. Forgetting his hair, he adjusted his positioning against the pole to plant his bare feet on the rocky ground. When he anchored himself to the ground, he dug his toes into the mud and rock to create a bond and extended his bound hands toward the sky. Then he pulled in a deep breath, settled his internal torment to open his mind and heart. Insight and openness are the keys to Goddess magic. Something he learned as a boy sitting by his grandmother. Over time, a deep sense of confidence settled within his body, knowing he was an essential part of the sacred cycles of life. He needed this confidence more than ever to survive this night.

"I call upon thee, beloved Triple Goddesses. Maiden, Mother and Crone, assist thy son of the ancient blood." He invoked the power of his magic and the energy piercing the tempest. "Blessed Crone's power, Dark Moon Hour, Fire to Banish and magic flow, bringeth the wisdom and energy to me. I called upon thee to make heat lightning happen in this place, here and now. Make the skies light up with this bright light. Oh, blessed goddess of nature, make haste and answer my pleas!"

Jagged forks of lightning speared to where he stood in defiance. Raw power forced into him, the entry piercing and harsh. He caressed and welcomed the bolt. It sizzled against wet flesh before it dissipated. The iron heated against his skin, caused his control of the magic to falter a bit. He fought against the increasing pain to hold onto the energy and break the cuffs.

Hidden within the thunder, Morric heard something move against the rocks. Swift and sure, heavy in weight, but delicate in movement. When another bolt lit the sky, he watched it illuminate a massive being. His control dropped, the energy dispersed in a gentle flow back to the earth.

"Beloved Triple Goddess, protect me."

Hues of midnight blue and ebony filled his view before he met a large single eye, the color of a brilliant rich emerald, scrutinizing his. Long lashes slid down over that orb before it pulled back. The flickers highlighted the long snout, the flare of nostrils.

Morric took in the rest of the creature's massive head complete with horns. "This is impossible..."

A puff of smoke enveloped him in a brief moment before it dissipated.

"Dragon..." he stuttered between trembling lips. "Perhaps there is some truth..." He yanked against the shackles.

A powerful front claw reached out with talons, longer than his forearms, sharpened to razor-edged points. Instead of ripping, slashing, spilling his blood, it enfolded him within a tender grasp. The shackles magically opened and dropped.

Morric couldn't see the rest of the body nor the wings that carried this creature aloft. The power needed to call down the lightning exhausted him and the shock took him over that last edge of consciousness. When his toes left the rock, he let out a gasp as darkness overwhelmed him.

Dragon. I saw a dragon.

Chapter Two

"Quite a strange sacrifice they've chosen to give on this stormy evening."

Drifting awake to the sensual tenor tone, Morric listened while he felt the calloused hand glide down his arm. Warmth flared against his back and hips. A strange calm overwhelmed him.

"Are you an innocent? You're not meek. Your body responds eagerly to my touch, even in sleep. It seems you prefer the touch of men. You can't hide the heft and thickness of your cock."

Breath teased a curl against Morric's neck. The stranger's hand trailed sensuously down his arm.

A calloused finger brushed one of his nipples. Morric felt his breathing quicken. His nipple hardened under the flicking touch. It had been so long since another man held him, touched him. If the town learned he preferred men, they would cry heresy and outrage for they declared a loving touch between men to be sin. They would kill him if they learned, so he remained alone all these years. How he missed another strong male body cradling him. He bit his lip to stifle the outcry of delight.

"Quite a different reaction from all the fair maidens. None of them reacted like this to my touch, my presence against them. Not you. Your body is coming alive under my touch," the man said, continuing to speak in a soft voice. "I know you're awake. I feel the rapid thud of your pulse.

Are you going to keep the pretense of staying asleep? Should I release my calming spell?"

Debating options, Morric opened his eyes at how the stranger mentioned using a spell upon him. "Are you using a spell?"

"Of course, otherwise the maidens screamed whenever I dare get close to them." A delightful chuckle rumbled through them. "Ahh, you're awake. Wonderful."

"I'm no damn maiden."

"Of course not. No maiden has this," the stranger said while he cupped Morric's thickening cock in his hand, "between their legs."

Morric grumped at how he played into this stranger's hands, but moved his legs to dislodge the tender grip. He felt the stranger's powerful frame shift away from him. Pushing up on one elbow, Morric looked around his new surroundings. A huge stone hearth filled with a fire burning. Settled on a pile of blankets, furs and a thick pad of some sort, Morric realized he was naked. His sodden clothes stripped from him. He pursed his lips together and glanced over his shoulder.

"Hello there," the man said.

Morric kept his gaze upon the forest green eyes surrounded by lush black lashes. The brilliant gaze set within a near perfect face hewn from pale marble. A lush sheen and fall of midnight black hair swirled around the stranger's forehead and over naked broad shoulders. His gaze bold while it lazily appraised him. He radiated vitality and power. There was a hint of magic around him.

"Such a lovely pair of eyes for a dragon's sacrifice. Endless blue like a spring sky. Who are you?" The stranger's thumb skimmed across Morric's cheekbone.

"Morric. Who are you to take such liberties with my body?"

"My name is Xavier. I'm servant and protector of the dragon's lair. I enjoy the keeping of sacrificial maidens."

"Again. I'm no maiden."

The man tilted his head back and laughed.

At the sound of the rich laughter, Morric felt a deep response quickening inside him. His body wanted this man. He couldn't let it happen. He wasn't a sacrifice.

There was something about those eyes.

Morric rolled further away. He snagged one of the blankets while he rose to his feet and covered himself with the cloth. He managed to work the length of fabric to wrap around his hips and secured with a simple tuck. It would have to do for now.

"That is a disappointing choice you have made, sacrifice. There's no need to cover yourself from my sight and touch," Xavier said while he sat up. A portion of his hair fell forward, covered half of his face, and shaded one of his eyes. With his movements, the blanket drifted to reveal wide shoulders, defined pectorals that slimmed to a flat abdomen. Dark curls arrowed down the middle of his body, bisected his perfection. The blankets pooled around his hips to hide the remaining portion of his body from Morric's sight.

"What about the dragon?"

"What about him?"

"Are we in its lair?"

"Yes, this is his home. I also reside here."

"Him?"

"The dragon is a male. They do have sexes."

"Of course," Morric said. "They? There is more than one?"

"More than anyone believes. Dragons keep to themselves, trying not to reveal themselves to humans unless absolutely necessary."

"Like a sacrifice?"

"Well. The dragon resided within these mountains long before that town."

These words changed everything Morric believed about dragons. *Sweet Maiden, this is crazy.* He scratched at the overnight growth on his chin. "Where is your dragon lord?"

"Hmm, he will be returning soon." Xavier held his hand out and beckoned Morric to return to the bed. "Please return to my side. We can pass this time in a more pleasant fashion. You have such an intoxicating scent of nature and lightning. I don't wish to wait for his return before exploring your delectable body."

Morric shook his head and took a few more steps back. The magic in the air buzzed around him. Xavier used some kind of compulsion spell, but Morric wasn't answering it.

Xavier narrowed his gaze at Morric's resistance.

Morric refused to budge. Not until he had his answers. "How long do you enjoy this keeping of a sacrifice?"

"Why are you so determined to find the answers in spite of the possibility of passion?"

"Please..."

"Do you not wish to feel my touch upon your body?"

"I want to know why I'm here."

Xavier rolled his eyes at Morric's continued insistence for answers. "You're the chosen sacrifice for the dragon so he'll suppress his violence against the town for the next equinox."

"This is the town's belief, but not the dragon. How does that work out?"

"Again, the dragon never asked for a sacrifice from anyone in his long life. Why should he bother with this small town and their archaic beliefs?"

"Yet, the dragon continues to take the sacrifices."

"He never asked for a sacrificial offering, but will not let a human suffer."

"Laws of a dragon?"

"A simple moral code," Xavier said in a sharp and clipped tone. "As for the length of time. It varies. The dragon determines the time of your stay based solely upon your character. I may persuade him to keep you longer."

"Why would the dragon share his bounty with you?"

"I'm his guardian."

"A human guardian for a dragon." Morric snorted. "I don't believe that. How did you end up in this position?"

"I'm the keeper of his lair. He entrusts me with everything."

"Are you his slave?"

"I'm no one's slave," Xavier said. His voice darkened. A rush of ancient energy snapped around him.

Cautious, Morric stepped back.

"For this decision and life at his side," Xavier continued in a calmer fashion, "he allows me to partake in the pleasures of a lover."

"The unwilling sacrifices."

"If that is the one in the lair, yes, and not all are unwilling. Most of the maidens are interested in having me as a lover. They're not as innocent as that town believes. Most aren't even true maidens, experienced in sexual matters, just not married. If they don't wish for this, then I'll make them comfortable until their time here is done." Xavier swept his hair back from his face.

"What about the dragon? What about his pleasures?"

"He can't enjoy the caress of a human's flesh."

"Caress. Sex. I don't understand. Why wouldn't he rip into me? Isn't this how a sacrifice works?"

"A little archaic for his tastes." Xavier shook his head. "Only savored and tasted by yours truly for the time of your entrapment."

"How long might that be?"

"We'll discuss that later." Xavier waved a hand to dismiss the question. "For now, dear Morric, I'm tired of this conversation. I desire for something more physical and pleasurable. It's been a while since the last equinox sacrifice. My hunger increased while watching you slumber." He studied Morric's body with blatant lust. "You're the first male sacrifice. I wonder why they chose you. It's quite an interesting change." He held out his hand and curled his fingers along with the brush of an increased compulsion spell. "Please, stop with all these questions. Come closer so we can enjoy some pleasure."

Planting his feet against the spell, Morric called a lightning ball to appear between his fingers. The white heat sizzled and sparked. "I don't think that will happen."

Xavier studied Morric's hand. He lifted an eyebrow and moved his stare back to Morric's face. "You're not from the town..."

Chapter Three

"What gave that little fact away?" Morric twisted and played with the flickering ball to show off a touch of his power and control. "If you're wondering, you would be correct."

"Which means you're not the sacrifice."

"Again, correct. Excellent to know we're coming to an understanding." Morric tilted his head a bit to indicate the magic. "Drop the spell. Now."

"You can sense magic."

"Aye, I can magic in more ways than you considered. Drop the spell. It's never going to work upon me. My shields are too strong."

"Interesting." Xavier flicked away something and shifted his position within the nest of blankets.

Morric no longer felt the desire to join the man.

"If you claim to not be the sacrifice then please sort out this issue," Xavier said with a deliberate pause. "Why were you on the precipice in white cotton and chained to the post?"

"Some of the townspeople drugged my tea, dragged me up there and left me. This wasn't my choice. The drug was tasteless and odorless. I didn't know what they did until I woke up."

"You were left for my dragon lord as his sacrifice."

"I'm no sacrifice. Not a volunteer or willing to fill the position. Ever." Morric sent a burst of energy to cause the sizzling lightning ball to flare up and flicker. "Do I look like a sacrifice? I'm no whimpering fool."

"Why would they leave you?"

Morric shrugged with a bare movement. He adjusted his grip on the blanket, hiked it back up one hip when he felt a breeze against his butt. The knot came loose at some point. "Does it matter? I was on the precipice when the dragon captured me. What does being a sacrifice mean? Death by claws? Cooked for the evening meal. Or sent on my way, spanked and used by the servant?"

Xavier narrowed his gaze. "That was rather nasty. I'm no servant."

"Keep telling yourself that and one day you might even believe those words," Morric snapped back. "I have no interest in staying with you or your damnable dragon lord. Oh, this is impossible. Make your master appear now!"

"He follows his own whims and timeframe. I can't call him like a dog."

Infuriated by Xavier's refusal and exasperating wanton behavior, anger rose within Morric and further ignited his gifts. He sent his lightning across the room and deep inside Xavier's body.

The thrust of energy sent Xavier flying across the room. The man crashed against the wall and dropped to the ground in a heap.

With the powerful distraction, Morric raced around to find a door. When there was no doorway in sight, he scrambled to the next wall for escape.

"There will be no escape for you, witch."

Morric slid to a stop. *No, this man was no servant. Nor was this man...a man.* He backed away until he hit another wall. He kept his gaze on the fearsome sight. "Oh, sweet Triple Goddess."

Huge black wings unfurled from Xavier's back and curled around his body. Bright light surrounded him before he rose in one fluid motion. He stood there, boldly intimidating, with vicious scorch marks across his pectorals from the lightning. The harsh red and white marks faded along with the swollen skin while he healed all of the damage. Talons extended from his fingers. Xavier's mouth curled in a snarl. A puff of gray smoke floated above him. His eyes brightened to a brilliant emerald.

The emerald color of Morric's dreams. His knees went jelly at the thought. He wobbled within the protective crouch, struggled to keep upright and pressed a hand against the wall. *Oh, dear sweet Maiden, don't let this be the meaning behind those dreams.*

"Witch..." Xavier rolled his shoulders and neck. Bones cracked and popped with the movement. The wings fluttered and flapped before folding against his back. "Now you can be my witch."

"Dragon. Some simple human guardian you claim to be," Morric taunted. The dragon's words stopped him. Anger locked his knees while he straightened from his protective crouch. "Your witch? I'm not your witch. Far from it." He would deny his dreams and their meaning. This wasn't his destiny. "Where do you hail from?"

"From an ancient magical line descended down since before the time of Camelot. I have seen much in my lifetime. More than you could ever imagine." Xavier flapped and refolding one wing. He lifted and rescinded the talons within his fingers. "What style of a witch are you?"

"A son of the McShayne family from the line of the ancient Fae."

"McShayne... Of course you would belong to that line."

"You know of my bloodline."

"Aye, I've met many of your ancestors. Your grandfather was a royal Fae. The last three generations of this line of elemental witches resided in the forest below my mountains."

Morric remained quiet, listening to the dragon.

"I knew the elders of your family, but they never caused any trouble during my ventures away from the lair. Until you. The last McShayne." Xavier's jeweled perusal stopped to connect to Morric's stare. "Now you stand within my mountain."

"Nor did I care to venture near your mountain. This wasn't my blasted decision!" Morric snapped back. "I was quite happy with my cottage and forest. I only wish to remain in the surroundings of my family's legacy. I never desired anything more than to remain with the earth and my work." Once again, he rolled his fingers and sent a snapping lightning ball towards the ceiling to burn off some anger. He paced in front of the wall, kicked the blanket away when it threatened to trip him. "Damnable. Insufferable. Superstitious. Fools! I swear the town will feel my vengeance."

Xavier's eyebrow soared to his hairline. He glanced at the vaulted ceiling. "Do watch the stalactites. They can become wicked sharp and not the thing you want to fall."

Morric glanced up to see the multiple tapering structures hanging like icicles from the roof of the cavern. These stalactites stopped dripping and producing the mineral precipitation for some time.

"Your forest? You're the current McShayne. Interesting." Xavier paced a moment. "How can this be happening? The magic quieted within the forest. The power lessened."

This time, Morric dropped his gaze to the floor. Pain rippled through him. He licked his lower lip and said, "My family passed into the next life."

"How can this be? Are you all that remains for the dances?"

"Haven't you been listening to me? Unbelievable."

"There could be other family members who are not gifted but witness the dance."

"No. There is no one else." Morric straightened his shoulders in an almost haughty fashion. He allowed his long hair to tumble carelessly down his back. "I'm the only McShayne! The last of the McShaynes. My mother passed two winters ago."

"What about the rest of the family? The last generation had six sisters, all with mates and families. You're one of those children of the youngest sister. There were two brothers, but not gifted."

"The town's encroachment and beliefs. Devastation reigned down upon my family. Three aunts fled with their families to try and protect the line. I never learned what happened to them or their children.

They're hidden from any visions or scrying," Morric said and rubbed his hand over his chest. Agony of the loss filled him with pain. "Disease killed another aunt and her family. Stress or outright repercussions by the town didn't help settle the matter. My aunt barely escaped with her life, unable to bear children. She is the last female. My sisters didn't survive childhood."

"What about—"

"There are no more McShaynes!" Morric shouted. Lightning flashed from his fingers at the pain and anger coursing through him from the loss of his family. "I do not lie with females so I'm the last. The end of my bloodline. Is that what you wish to hear? How I'm alone to hold my family's legacy, to keep my forest safe and alive?" He turned to stare at Xavier, forced the tears to not fall, but felt them burn. Every single time he danced alone, another rip tore into his heart at the aching loss of his family.

While flexing his arms out, his muscles bunched and relaxed, Xavier recalled the wings back to him. He popped a couple more vertebrae to let out the rest of his anger. The echo of the hollow sound bounced around in the growing silence between them. He glanced at his chest and rubbed a hand against his skin. "Forgive me, son of the McShayne bloodline. Condolences on the loss of your family, a beloved magical bloodline. It will truly be missed from this world." He placed a hand against his chest and bowed his head toward Morric.

Morric blinked at the unexpected apology. "Thank you."

Xavier looked around them and at his nudity. Comfortable in it, he rubbed his hands together. "This has been an unexpected evening. Not what usually happens."

"How so?"

"Usually I get through my time with a sacrifice without revealing secrets, but you took matters in your own hands.

"You gave me no choice."

"Should have realized something was different the moment you resisted the calming spell. Let alone your sex. They never offered a male sacrifice. Set me off guard." Xavier shrugged and paced a bit. A light flush colored his pale flesh. "Please forgive my behavior. I believe we got off on the wrong—"

"Wrong side of the bed?" Morric finished, giving him an easy out.

"A little worse, but I'll accept it." Xavier held out his hands in an offering, but brought them back to his sides. "How about I step away for a while? We can both decompress and regroup."

"Why?"

"I'll let you rest and recover from all that happened to you. We can speak further after your rest. You could tell me what happened to bring you to my lair."

"Do you offer this to other sacrifices?"

"Sometimes. All depends on the person." Xavier motioned between them. "This situation is vastly different. Everything that happened from the moment of your rescue. I don't wish to upset you further."

"You could release me."

"I don't think it would be wise. If the townspeople discovered you back at your cabin—" Xavier trailed off.

"They could kill me and someone else would be sacrificed."

"At the very least. Please, stay and be welcomed in my home."

Morric looked around the rather decadent lair. "Do I sleep here?"

"Ahh, perhaps best not. This chamber truly belongs to me when I'm in this form. My dragon form requires a much larger space, but I enjoy the comforts offered to my human form."

"Soft blankets or hard rock."

"And a couple of other items I've gathered over the centuries, but that's the general gist of the idea."

"Don't blame you. Then what about me? In the bowels of the mountain. A cot and straw?"

Xavier laughed and shook his head. "No. No. I have nothing of that nature around here. I toss my enemies off the top of the mountain."

Morric's eyes widened in a quick, sharp fashion.

Xavier laughed again. "Sorry. I couldn't resist."

"Right. I'm sure there's another unfortunate end for them."

"At times." Xavier swept a hand through his hair.

"Where do I go then?"

"Oh, sorry. I offer another chamber to all my guests. You can reside there for your time here. Clothing is available. Follow one of the hallways to the communal hot-spring bathing pool."

"I would appreciate that," Morric said.

Xavier walked around the room. He waved his fingers in front of a wall and doors opened to reveal a closet of sorts. He selected two dressing gowns and pulled on one. He closed the doors and returned to Morric's side. He held out the deep blue colored robe. "Perhaps this will be more comfortable than a blanket. Though I don't mind the view it offers." He tilted his head to peruse Morric's back.

"My ass is showing again. Isn't it?"

"Parts of it. Quite delectable."

Morric flushed. "Interesting spell with the wall," he said to try and redirect Xavier's attention. When Xavier blinked and smiled, he knew damn well the diversion didn't help. *Sweet Maiden, help me through this.* With the muttered prayer, he took the robe, slid his arms into the sleeves and secured the tie before he let the blanket tumble to the ground. "Thank you."

"Welcome. The color suits the blue in your eyes."

"Can't help yourself."

"A natural flirt and I've been a bit lonely," Xavier said with a smile.

"No excuse to grope someone without their permission."

"My apologies, son of McShayne. Never again without your permission." Xavier bowed low, but had the same smile upon his face. He opened a different door carved within the stone and led Morric there. "Follow me, please."

Chapter Four

Once left alone in the smaller chamber, Morric dropped heavily on the pile of blankets. He lowered his head in his hands. His head pounded from the overload on the sleeping draught. Then he'd called lightning while surrounded with iron. His body wasn't too happy with him.

Turning, he slid under the pile of soft blankets. This wasn't a typical bed with a frame, but some style of thick mattress upon the stone with blankets and sheets covering it. Either way, it was far more comfortable than his simple bed at home.

His eyes closed and he drifted into sleep easier than he imagined. His dreams quiet other than a brief flicker of piercing emerald eyes gazing upon him.

Some unknown time later, Morric awoke and stretched. Remembering the mention of a hot-spring pool, he rose and went in search of the communal area. The tumbling and bubbling sounds of the spring led him through the slight maze. Steam skimmed across the top while the water bubbled and frothed.

There was a pile of fluffy towels, a tray of different cleansing options, and candles flickering for a bit of light. The area comforted his jagged nerves.

Morris let the robe fall to the stone and slid into the pool. He moved into a deeper area of the pool until he could slip under the water. A little more centered, he rose out of the water. Where he stood, the water hit him a little below mid-chest. Water sluiced down his shoulder length hair and body. After he swiped both hands across his face and through his hair, he blinked open his eyes and moved back toward the edge to use the cleansing materials.

The cleanser was a silky liquid-gel material with a light fragrance of natural oils and herbs. It foamed easily under his fingers while he worked it through his hair. He poured another pile onto a puffy sponge-like object and scrubbed the liquid over his body.

Delighted by the cleanser and water, Morric took advantage of enjoying a decent bath in warm water. His regular options were either the chilly stream or a pitiful amount of water sloshing in a small tub heated by the fireplace. Baths were never a luxurious moment. He could definitely learn to enjoy this piece of his... Could he call it an imprisonment?

While he certainly hadn't volunteered to become a prisoner, chained to a pole in the middle of a thunderstorm, and captured by a dragon, the outcome wasn't what he expected. The dragon certainly wasn't expected. A myth. An ancient legend of his ancestors befriending a dragon when they first arrived within the forest.

This dragon.

Xavier.

His great-grandparents met this dragon.

How odd it came full circle for the last of the McShaynes held captive by the same dragon?

Fate?

Is this what the Triple Goddess wove into his destiny? Why else would they send him dreams of the dragon's emerald eyes and tenor voice whispering "mate" to him?

When his body responded to those thoughts, Morric moved the nubby sponge down his chest and belly. He soaped and fondled his thickening length and balls. While pleasure rolled through his body at his familiar touch, Morric tilted his head back. A soft hum rumbled up his throat. He continued to squeeze and pull on his cock, drawing the length through his increasing grip, calling his orgasm up from its hiding place.

While he worked his cock, he fondled and played with the sac. He pressed his finger against his taint and drew it back until he reached his ass. The slickness of the cleanser let him slip easily into the puckered entrance.

Curling slightly around to ease the movements, Morric worked his body. He knew the rhythm and motions required to bring him to orgasm.

The memories of Xavier's hands moving across his body rose. His nipples hardened under the ghost touch of calloused fingers. The tenor voice whispering decadent words in his ear. A warm breath against his neck.

Those eyes. Those emerald green eyes bright against the ebony lashes.

With the soft exhalation of Xavier's name, the orgasm broke and flooded his senses. Harsher and intense, Morric cried out with the pleasure-pain racing through him. He spurted ropes of seed into the water. His body spasm under his touch while his balls drained their essence.

Exhausted, he released his touched and drifted into the water. The bubbling waves rinsing his body of sex and cleanser. Morric tried to remember how to breathe.

"Oh. I didn't expect this. I apologize—"

The sound of a deliberate sniff yanked Morric's attention back to reality. He spun in the water to see Xavier draped in his robe and standing on the opposite side of the pool, having entered the area from his chambers.

Xavier smiled and licked his lower lip. "I know that scent."

Morric flushed and dipped further under the water. Embarrassment flooded him by being caught masturbating after turning away Xavier's earlier offer.

"Would have wished to witness such an event, but," Xavier said and shrugged. "Oh well. Do you mind if I join you?" Xavier opened the robe and let it fall to the stone. His cock resting against his thigh within a nest of ebony curls. Nonchalant in his nudity, he stretched his body. "Enjoyed a nap and need a bit of a refresher. I'll go about putting together a meal next." He went to the set of cut-in steps and descended into the water.

"Just finishing up." Morric ducked down to rinse his hair in the water. Rising to take a breath, he blinked open his eyes and found Xavier standing closer.

"No need to rush." Xavier lowered his gaze down Morric's body. With a knowing smile, he half-swim half-walked toward the cleansing options. "Do you enjoy the water?"

"It's a luxurious pleasure I'm not accustomed to having back in my cabin."

"Your cabin. Right, your home within the forest. Could you tell me exactly what happened which ended with you chained to the post in the storm as a sacrifice? I would like to know what happened to you."

Morric shoved a hand through his hair. He lowered further in the water, kicked his legs to make sure his seed disappeared completely. "Someone from the town watched my sky-clad lunar dance to welcome in the vernal equinox and refresh the land as my family has always done every season. Only this time, when I went to the town for a meeting, members of the town council drugged my tea. The drug wasn't something I would make or use and I couldn't taste or smell any difference. I should have been more careful, but I dropped my guard. I awoke to find myself shackled to the post in the middle of the storm." Morric rubbed his lower jaw.

"Irrational fools!" Xavier smacked the water a bit. "They don't know what magic they hinder. Without you, the forest will wither, as will their farms."

"The elders poured all their archaic beliefs into the dragon's sacrifice to protect their crafts and called my natural touch with the land evil and in league with the devil. Yet, they continued to barter with me for potions and teas amongst other items. Believe what you wish. I kept to my lands unless I had to go into town, but I didn't care for it."

Xavier bowed his head and murmured a dark curse. "They could have killed you."

"Instead they sent me to you. The one being who could understand me."

"I wish I could express how sorry I am about how you lost your home."

"I hope I didn't lose it completely and we can find a way to save my land. The land shouldn't die because some people hate me."

"I'll do whatever I can to figure out a way to protect your forest."

Morric bobbed a little within the water, the natural buoyancy of the spring holding his body. "This spring is wonderful, so soothing. Is this a natural spring?"

"I discovered this place within this series of caverns when I first surveyed the mountain. It helped make my decision to remain here. It's a free-flowing system from filling this cavity to emptying down a different drain of sorts. Same with the toiletry area. Keeps things refreshed, cleansed, and disease free."

"Can dragons become ill?"

"Sometimes, but it's difficult. We're immune to most human illnesses, but some can bother us within this form. It's miserable when a dragon sneezes."

"Fire and mucus don't mix?"

"Exactly. Gum up the works."

Morric laughed. He couldn't stop himself. When Xavier brushed against him, Morric's laughter quieted and he lifted his gaze. He met the emerald stare. A hint of honey and gold flickered within the emerald. Unlike humans, Xavier didn't have a dark shadow along his jaw. Other than the curls around his cock, Xavier's skin was devoid of any body hair.

Needing to touch and understand, Morric skimmed his fingers down Xavier's arm.

Xavier hummed under his breath. Warmth radiated from him. Morric wondered if steam would rise from either the water or the dragon with an orgasm.

"You have no body hair except for down there," Morric said.

"Transformation from scales to skin is a bit different and complicated."

"Why only that section?"

Xavier lifted an eyebrow. "No one has ever been so inquisitive around me. In all these centuries, I've never had to answer so many personal questions."

"Should I stop?"

"No. No. I find it odd, but..."

"But?"

"Not quite sure how to put it." Xavier shrugged when he paused. "Perhaps it's close to being grateful someone is paying attention to me. I've been in the shadows for so long."

"Or hiding behind a fake human persona."

"Don't know how well a sudden transformation from this form to human would go along with the other sacrifices?"

"Wouldn't want to watch it myself. I predict lots of high-pitched screaming or fainting or things being thrown around."

Xavier floated away and lowered his gaze to the water. "Many fear what they don't understand."

"I would like to understand you. And dragons."

"Only because I'm half forcing you to stay put."

"You made an excellent point of the town killing me if I return home. Something else will have to be done for the forest and my cabin."

"Or the town."

Morric waved a finger at Xavier as if he would scold a child. "No. Bad dragon. No setting the town on fire."

"Spoilsport," Xavier said with a half-smile.

"Though I hate the entire place, there are some good people there. The collection as a whole is rotten to the core, but some are good."

"Hard to pull out the good ones."

"Correct. No fires."

"Very well," Xavier said. "Back to the personal questions then."

"Do you mind? Truly? I'll stop if my inquiries bother you."

"Ask away."

Morric pointed down into the water. "Why hair there?"

A flush mottled Xavier's upper chest and neck. "In dragon form, our...ermm...privates are tucked inside a special pocket of sorts. The skin is softer, no scales, and a light covering of downy hair. The area reverses in this form."

"Really?"

"Kind of hard to fly around with a... umm..." Xavier rubbed the back of his neck while the flush darkened. The sex-craved flirt from earlier was gone. "My cock hanging down. Messes up the aerodynamics of flight."

"Would be rather uncomfortable," Morric said and smothered more chuckles at Xavier's fumbling. "You weren't this shy earlier." He drilled his finger into Xavier's side.

Xavier yelped and chuckled when Morric tickled a spot. He slid away from Morric's touch and batted his hand away. The flush disappeared while a playful expression filled his gaze. "Another subject."

"Not gonna touch that? Hmm?"

"Please."

Morric wiggled his fingers but stopped when Xavier captured them and brought them back under the water before letting go. Accepting the silent request, he sorted through his mental list of questions. "Your eyes. I noticed the color changes. When I awoke, your eyes were a forest green, darker in color. Now they're emerald. When your dragon rose, there were sparks of gold and honey." Morric skimmed his fingers down the side of Xavier's face.

Xavier became still under Morric's touch, barely moving within the water. "Glamour to keep up the pretense. Why maintain the unnecessary energy when you know the truth? The gold colors go along with my dragon's magic. Happens to other dragons, but in different shades that ranges across all precious metals. Our eyes are often some form of precious jewels or stones, more brilliant than human."

"Do you have glamour like Fae?"

"We came from the same ancestry and magic. Ancient times. There are legends and myths, but most of the knowledge is lost. You have Fae blood and magic. From your maternal grandfather, who was a full blood Royal Fae. Not the next in line for a throne, but high up in the Solas Court."

"It's the same with my paternal lineage. My father was half-Fae."

"Truly?"

Morric nodded.

"Hmm. Interesting mixture of bloodlines. Your magic recognized mine, a reason why my spells don't work. And your lightning ball did some damage."

"Please allow me to apologize for what happened—"

Xavier shook his head to interrupt Morric's apology. "No need for it. You defended yourself against my unwanted actions. I deserved a little ass-kicking."

"A little?"

Xavier held up both hands to give Morric the point. "A lot. Bad dragon."

Morric smirked. He floated away for a bit.

"Any more questions, concerns, comments?" While he pumped some of the silky foam into his palm, Xavier watched Morric partially float in the warm bubbly water. He rubbed his hands together and brought them to his hair.

"Why did you choose these mountains?"

"The territory was abundant with game and resources. It's close to the ocean. I enjoy taking a dip into the cool waters or playing along the surf. Either human or dragon. The climate is a comfortable mix of all the seasons. No other dragon claimed the area."

"How far away are we from the town and my forest?"

"Up the coast. It would take a human about a two-day ride or a little over a week's walk to reach the base of the mountains. There are many paths and caverns twisting all around these mountains and my dwelling is closer to the cliff face. It's easier to enter as a dragon and keeps away uninvited guests."

"Closer than I imagined. How large is your territory?"

"Hmm. On the far northern edge of your forest, which continues up the mountains. As for size, well, haven't quite measured it. In dragon form, I know it takes about a five moon cycles flight in any direction."

"Can you fly pretty far as a dragon?"

"Don't need to stop for much rest or other needs. With a good updraft, I can soar for a decent length of time and distance."

"Not being too specific."

"Need to keep some secrets," Xavier said with a grin before he ducked under the water to rinse.

Morric waited until Xavier rose and swept back the ebony locks from his face. "Are you alone? I mean..."

"Am I lonely?"

"Not including the sacrifices."

"Don't really think of them as decent company," Xavier said with a snort.

"That bad?"

"Sometimes. There are times I feel lonely, but dragons are solitary in nature. We rarely gather in large groups. Every century in the late fall, the females will select a sire for their next brood. It's one of the few times we'll gather for the mating calls."

"Have you been selected?"

"A couple of times, but I never met the dragonets, which is customary. Of course, it's rare for an entire brood to survive hatching and youngling years. Not many make it to maturity, another unfortunate fact of our kind." While he spoke, Xavier made quick work of scrubbing his body and rinsing the suds from his skin.

"Have you met any of your offspring?"

"I suspect I recognized a few of my offspring during the ritual gatherings, but I don't intrude. An offspring can come to us if they desire to learn more about their parentage." Xavier moved closer, the water barely rippling around him. "Do you really wish to discuss this with me?"

"Though I desire you, I will not share your bed," Morric said.

Xavier traced a finger along Morric's cheekbone. "Can't."

"Will not. There is a difference."

"Not while I keep your freedom and forest from you."

Morric looked away, turned his head, unable to look upon Xavier.

"I see. I do this only to protect you from certain death. Even you realized what could happen if you return. An answer to this problem will appear to us. Give it time."

"Until then, I don't believe it's wise to share your bed."

"Understood." Xavier placed his finger upon Morric's chin to turn him back toward him. "May I have one request?"

"What is it?"

"A kiss. Just a kiss."

Suddenly, Xavier's mouth covered Morric's before he could answer. His mouth was moist, tender and wonderful.

Morric groaned under the gentle onslaught. He buried his hands in Xavier's wet hair. Tilting a bit for another angle, he let the kiss go on for some time. His mouth thoroughly explored and devoured.

Something crackled and sizzled.

Flickers of pale blue fire surrounded them. Heat and power flashed into Morric, snapping his spine straight to make him pull back with a cry. Darkness swept over him while he gasped for breath.

When he came back, a cloud of pure white smoke ringed over them.

Xavier cradled him, having moved them toward the cut-in stairs.

Morric cleared his throat twice. His mouth dry. Somehow, he managed to find his voice. "What happened?"

"Something unexpected. I'm so sorry. I never thought this would happen."

There was panic in Xavier's voice.

Morric focused his fuzzy gaze upon Xavier. He felt Xavier move his hold until he lifted Morric out of the water. He took hold of Xavier's shoulders to hang onto him while Xavier brought him back to the guest chamber. No one had carried him around since he was a child.

Xavier settled him on the bundle of mattress and blankets. He covered Morric with one of the lighter blankets. "Rest. I'll bring food. I must—" He stopped and straightened while he took a few steps back. He dragged fingers through his hair.

"What happened to me, Xavier?"

"I can't explain now. Please. I must—"

"Xavier?"

Shaking his head, Xavier spun and hurried out of the chamber.

Morric pushed up on one hand. "Xavier!"

Too exhausted to follow the dragon racing away from him, his magic buzzing in an unusual way, Morric dropped back to the mattress. Soon, he slid into sleep.

Chapter Five

Lost in the gray fathoms of unconsciousness, Morric twitched but couldn't budge. His magic buzzed and burned within him. A wild bright blue rope of magic twined around him, danced with his magic in some kind of eternal courtship or battle.

Morric, my witch, return to me. Please...

Groggy, Morric knew that tenor tone with a bit of rasp.

Xavier.

Xavier called to him.

Something grabbed him and pulled him back under the building fog.

Morric, please, do not leave me. Return to me.

Once again, Xavier's voice tugged at him. The blue rope continued to twine and dance. Something happened deep within him, but he couldn't figure out what was occurring. He never experienced anything like this when it came to using his witchcraft.

Morric. Dear witch.

The fog's tendrils drew him back under, away from Xavier's pleas.

Sometime later, Morric climbed his way out of the deep sleep. His back twitched and itched. He had no idea how long he'd been under. Every bone in his body ached and this told him he had slept for some time.

"What happened to me?" he muttered in a raspy tone. "Xavier?" He rubbed a hand over his face and looked around the room. There was no sign of the dragon. He swore he heard Xavier call to him. Taking great care not to jostle his aching head, he curled to a sitting position.

The blankets fell around his waist, revealing he was naked once again. The last memory was Xavier carrying him out of the springs and straight to the chambers. There hadn't been a thought to dress him, or even let him dry from the extended bathing time.

Morric pressed a hand against his aching head. The twitch and itch sensations continued to flare and ripple across his back.

Turning to put his feet on the covered stone floor, Morric tested his strength and balance. When he managed to stand straight, he moved to one of the walls. After watching Xavier, Morric learned what to look and feel for with his magic. He tapped the right spot to make the rock open and reveal the hidden closet.

A full-length tri-fold mirror expanded when Morric pulled open both doors. He grimaced at his haggard appearance. Pale from the extended sleep and little food, he scratched at his chin. As usual, his jaw remained smooth. For some reason he never could grow a decent beard let alone deal with the overnight scruff. He couldn't quite figure out why, but kind of grateful he didn't need to shave every morning.

Something dark caught his eye in the reflection from the far mirror.

"What in the name of the Crone?" Morric twisted until he could see his entire back within the reflections. "Blessed Triple Goddess, how can this be?"

A massive black dragon with emerald eyes and runes stretched from the nape of his neck to just above his ass. He contorted his arm to touch the image to figure out how it appeared on his skin. There was no ink or scarring. Nothing to explain its sudden appearance upon his skin.

Xavier.

The blue fire.

What had Xavier done to him?

Lightning sparks flickered from his fingers. It was time he had a good talk with the damnable dragon.

Morric stepped into a pair of pants, the fabric smooth and silky, and selected a different robe in a warm cream, the material thin and soft. He buttoned the few buttons to cover his chest. The remaining part of the robe opened and flowed around his lower body, the fabric finer than anything he'd ever worn. This time he could see the exquisite embroidery decorating the sleeves and lapels.

After closing the closet, Morric moved to another wall to find the other hidden door. This one opened to a hallway different from the one leading to the hot springs. The stone was warm and smooth under his bare feet while he followed multiple paths.

One path led him to a kitchen of sorts. His empty belly growled and snarled from having next to nothing. Morric didn't feel any guilt when he raided the cold storage and pantry to put together a nourishing meal. He didn't keep track how many glasses of cool spring water he drank until the dry feeling settled. Belching several times after being gluttonous to clear the excess air that he gulped with the water and food, Morric finally felt satisfied. At least when it came to food. He placed the dishes in the sink to wash later.

With that need taken care of, Morric set off to locate Xavier. He had to be somewhere within this maze.

The thunderous sounds of waves breaking against rock grew louder. Morric headed toward the sound, letting it guide him through this labyrinth. Rounding a long corner, Morric entered a massive cavern. Larger than anything he found along his walk.

At the far end, daylight and a blue sky appeared bright against the surrounding stone.

Morric stepped forward and lifted his face when a fresh breeze caressed his skin. "Blessed Triple Goddess, that feels wonderful." With those words and the feel of the wind, Morric realized he hadn't offered prayers to the Goddess since his awakening during the massive storm. He felt ashamed, but the need to find Xavier remained firm in his mind.

Moving across the expansive cavern, he caught a glimmer of a magical barrier stretched across one corner. It looked like there was another wall, but it wasn't solid. He held out his hands to figure out this protective shield. The glistening barrier snapped and cracked against his fingers but parted to allow him entrance.

Instead of an empty cavern, he stepped into a massive annex. High up on the walls, cauldron-type containers filled with roaring fires lit up the annex. Piles of glimmering shiny gold in all shapes and sizes, glittering precious gems and stones, and leather-bound books filled most of the area. The books were stacked neat in some sort of order. The gold and jewels left haphazardly around.

Crouching, Morric scooped up the closest golden coins. He flipped through them, noticing the distinctive stamps from multiple countries and realms.

Coins slid down one pile, tinkling and tingling while they hit, rolled, and spilled.

Morric went around the impressive pile.

Curled against the backside of the pile, facing away from the cavern's entrance, was the massive ebony dragon. Powerful wings tucked against his sides and back. Like a cat, the dragon flicked his long tail in a restless beat. Each swish sent more coins spilling down the pile.

Unlike the night of the storm, Morric could study the large head. A series of horns started behind the eye ridges and continued down through the upper neck until it reached the shoulders. Small tufted ears folded back against the scales. The long snout with the powerful jaws and teeth rested so close to Morric. He could touch the shiny scales without moving another step. The ebony scales glistened under the flames and revealed a touch of blue and silver. Each scale shaped perfectly to create the protective hide. Some said nothing could pierce a dragon's hide.

The nostrils flared when they captured Morric's scent. A puff of smoke rose from one nostril and disappeared.

The dragon lifted his massive head higher, shook a bit, and opened his eyes. There was Xavier. Within those glistening emerald eyes. In either dragon or human form, Morric would forever recognize those eyes.

"Quite a hoard you have in here. Didn't expect to find all this when I came searching for you," Morric said. He opened his hand that still held the coins. He bounced the coins to make them flip a couple of times. Then he threw them away to join the treasured hoard.

Xavier tilted his head to get a better angle to see Morric.

"Can you speak in this form?"

/only like this but it hurts mortals/ Xavier spoke within Morric's mind.

Morric winced because it did cause a bit of a headache.

/I apologize but I sought the serenity of dragon form while you continued the deep sleep/ Xavier continued.

Morric massaged his temples with his fingers. "Could you please transform? We need to talk about what happened."

Xavier looked away.

"Please, Xavier. Don't deny me this." Morric stepped closer and touched the elongated forearm, which ended in a paw and powerful talons. He stroked the scales and found them smooth as glass. "I'm a little scared about what is going on and I need answers. You're the only one with them."

/give me a moment/ Xavier said. */please step back/*

Morric moved away from Xavier.

Within moments, the massive dragon form shrank and collapsed upon itself. While there was magic involved, it seemed something else made this transformation happen. There were snaps, pops, and creaks of bone and muscle reshaping. When it ended, Xavier's golden-skinned human form crouched where the dragon once rested. A sheen of sweat glistened his skin and dampened his hair.

Morric looked around and discovered the magical spot to open a closet. He raced over, touched the spot to open the wardrobe doors. He took out a lush, luxurious robe. After closing them, he went to where Xavier remained crouched.

Xavier's breathing was a bit raspy and quickened. Until he pushed against the floor and rose to his full height. He shook out his limbs, something rippled under the skin, while he grimaced and let everything continue to redistribute.

"Are you all right? I didn't expect the transformation to be quite so visceral," Morric said to give more time for Xavier to recover.

"Did you expect a cloud, sparkles and poof the dragon disappears and a man appears?"

"Something like that."

"I'm not a magic act." Xavier grimaced and tilted his head far to the right. A couple of the mid-neck vertebrae popped loud and nasty. "Ouch. Hellfire."

Morric winced at the noise. "What..."

"My bones settling into place." Xavier grimaced again and rolled a shoulder backwards for another loud *pop*. "Some more reluctant than others." He accepted the robe from Morric, slid his arms into the sleeves and tied the front in place. After he shoveled his fingers through his hair, he gave Morric a smile. "Greetings and hello."

Morric tilted his head at the old-fashioned greeting. "Hello."

Xavier caressed Morric's face. "You're awake."

"How long have I been out?"

"Two moons passed. The waning crescent moon will rise tonight. I remained by your bedside throughout the day, dribbled water onto your lips to keep you hydrated, and spoke to you, but received no response. At night, I slid into dragon form because I wanted to be curled around you, do whatever I could to wake you, but—" Xavier lowered his gaze.

"I told you I didn't want to share your bed."

"I took it to mean everything. I'm sorry," Xavier said. Shame filled his expression. "I should have gone with my instincts and stayed with you no matter what time of day or night."

"You didn't stay away completely. I heard you."

"What?"

"I heard you while trapped within the fog. Your voice calling to me."

"Oh. I became so worried about your health that I sent for a healer."

"What about a healer? Where would you find one?"

"From the Fae since a mortal healer doesn't know magic and you're of the bloodline. There's an entrance to the land of the Fae within the mountains."

"The Fae are here?"

"They created an opening to their land within the mountain. The gate opens within the Timeless Forest, the barrier between the Solas and Dorcha courts."

"Why is there a barrier?"

"The Dorcha court remains in eternal winter while the Solas court maintains eternal summer. The Forest cycles through all four seasons. When winter and summer cycle are in the Forest, the courts come together for a grand celebration."

"Have you been to these celebrations?"

"When I've been invited, I joined them. Lots of music, dancing, feasting and drinking. Then there is courting between the younglings. Then there are all the political discussions and maneuvers among the nobles, royals and guards."

"How did you come to meet the Fae?"

"When I chose these my mountains for my home, I offered to help secure and protect their entrance. Not many try to get past a pissed off dragon."

"What kind of Otherkin are around here? What have I missed by staying within my forest?"

"Along with the dragons and Fae, there are elves, merpeople, and dwarves. Dwarves are only found in the northernmost mountains and remain deep underground to mine and explore. They rarely go aboveground. Clusters of merpeople are in both oceans and some of the deep natural lakes. There's a lake on the far side of these mountains with a colony. Elves share land with the Fae, but have their own courts and kingdoms."

"I didn't know so many continued to live."

"Otherkin learn to blend with the humans. It's imperative, but some humans, like your family, sense the Otherkin. Bloodlines can and do intermingle."

"What did you tell the Fae about me?"

"I explained who you were and what happened. They were most eager to meet you due do your Fae heritage," Xavier said. "They planned to send someone. I expect them before the sun set."

"But I'm awake." Morric stopped and remembered the image on his back. "What happened to me?"

"There is much to explain, but—" Xavier paused when the air pressure altered just enough to pop their ears.

"What the—"

"The Fae. They can create a magical portal into my mountain. I gave them permission," Xavier said. He placed his hand against Morric's lower back and guided him back toward the main entrance cavern.

A section of the mountain swirled onto itself into a decent size oval. Sparkles of magic filtered within the swirls.

Chapter Six

Morric could only stare in amazement at a sight he never thought to witness.

A tall, lean figure stepped out of the portal.

The male wore long silver robes, wielded a walking staff with a brilliant white jeweled nestled within the caged top, and had a large bag slung across his body. His silvered brown hair slicked back from his forehead, with the upper section gathered into a rope with multiple ties down the length. The rest hung straight down to his mid-back. His face elegant, defined cheekbones led up to the pointed ears. A silver pendant hung from his neck. Morric recognized the pendant was fashioned into the symbol of healing and medicine for the Fae.

Following the robed figure was another equally tall and elegant male. This one wore tight leggings and knee-high boots in chocolate leather, a pewter gray shirt billowed around his arms and chest with a thigh-length chocolate embroidered and bejeweled vest. His golden hair pulled back into a double set of ropes with multiple ties. A golden circlet of vines and leaves rested upon his forehead. Forever battle ready, a full quiver rested against his back with a long bow, daggers, and a sheathed sword along his leg. His bi-colored sapphire gaze focused on Morric and Xavier.

"Prince Caderyn of the Golden Forest Fae, greetings and welcome to my home. I didn't expect you to accompany Healer Diarmid," Xavier said and bowed deep to the prince. "I wish to present to you the witch I found as an unexpected sacrifice, Morric McShayne."

Morric glared a second at Xavier, who winked back. He turned to the prince, pressed his clasped fist to his chest and bowed in respect to the Fae prince. "Greetings and welcome."

"You're not the McShayne witch who ventured into my father's court," the prince said. His tone and speech eloquent and similar to Xavier.

Not moving when he heard those words, Morric trembled while some crazy feeling like hope flitted through his veins.

"Not the best way to introduce yourself, my prince," the healer said.

Xavier touched Morric's hand. "Morric—"

"A McShayne witch? When? Where?" Morric sent the questions rapid fire.

The prince lifted one eyebrow high at the idea of someone questioning him. "Aye, a male witch. Dark hair. Same blue eyes. I don't know how he entered our realm and found his way to Court."

"Male—" Morric leaned against Xavier when the idea of another McShayne witch overwhelmed him. "Do you know his name?"

"Nay. He disappeared before I could question him. The bloodline magic runs true through both of you. He's of your line," the prince said.

Morric twisted his hand to grip Xavier's hand. Hard. He wasn't alone. He wasn't the last.

"Perhaps now would be a suitable time for us to move to a more comfortable area to converse," the healer said.

"Of course. Follow me," Xavier said while he wrapped one hand around Morric's waist to support him and let him cling to his other hand.

He gestured to the others to follow him and led them through the labyrinthine passages. The opening revealed a completely different cavern filled with long plush sofas filled with pillows and blankets. Low tables and those odd cauldrons of fire finished the area along with pieces of artwork.

"Every cavern is different. How many rooms are here?" Morric looked around while they stepped further in the room.

"I haven't counted in a while. I don't use many of them, but kept a set clustered together." Xavier brought Morric to the closest sofa and helped him sit down. "Please have a seat. Would either of you like a cup of tea?"

"Perhaps one of my herbal mixtures for Morric would be best," the healer said while he sat down. He brought the strap over his head and dug inside to pull up a small bound pouch. "This one should help. A few calming herbs." He named some of the herbs within the mix.

"I create something similar," Morric said.

"Excellent. Xavier, a pot of hot water and cups. I can offer everyone something different to brew."

With a nod, Xavier crouched next to Morric, who continued to cling to his hand. He pushed back a lock of Morric's hair. "I'm not going far. I promise. You're safe with them."

Lifting his gaze, Morric met Xavier's perusal. "I'll steady myself. A bit of a shock."

"Healer Diarmid, Morric woke up a couple of hours ago from the deep sleep I mentioned. If he agrees, could you check him over?" Xavier asked.

"Of course," Diarmid said and looked to Morric. "Would you allow this?"

Morric nodded. He released his tight grip on Xavier's hand.

"Excellent. I'll return in a moment," Xavier said before he left the room.

Morric watched him leave.

"Our Xavier is protective of a witch. Quite interesting," Diarmid said.

At Diarmid's voice, Morric turned to the Fae. "Your Xavier?"

"Our ancestry has the same origins. We've been his closest family since his arrival centuries ago to our lands," the prince said while he remained standing. He crossed his arms and studied Morric. "He hasn't revealed his true nature to anyone. How did you learn of his identity?"

"He pissed me off and I shot a lightning ball at him," Morric said, figuring he better go for the truth around the Fae.

"A lightning ball? Can you summon that much power within the stone?"

"Normally, I would say no, but I called the storm and lightning to me when I tried to free myself from the shackles. The residual power remained within me when I woke up somewhere in one of the chambers," Morric said.

Diarmid chuckled. "Did he try his flirtatious routine with you?"

"A little further than flirting."

Diarmid chuckled harder. "Those mundane sacrifices haven't given him any sort of sport or decent conversation. He's became rather stuck in a rut, you might say."

"Until you came along," the prince added.

When he controlled his humor, Diarmid rose and settled next to Morric. "May I perform a simple scan? I'll not intrude upon your mind or magic."

The prince wandered around the room and stopped short when he was behind Morric and the sofa. "I don't believe a scan will be necessary. I can see the complication. Does Xavier know what happened to you?"

Morric shook his head. "Haven't gotten the chance to talk to him."

"What do you see, Caderyn?" Diarmid asked.

"He's been marked with Xavier's magic."

"Marked?"

"Morric, could you stand and remove the robe? Diarmid, you need to look what's upon his back."

Morric glanced between the Fae. The dragon image.

"If Caderyn is correct, this changes everything," Diarmid said while he stood. "Rise, please. Remove the robe."

"Is this bad?"

"I must study the image first," Diarmid said.

With a long sigh, Morric rose while he unbuttoned the robe. He shrugged his shoulders to let the thin fabric slip down his arms and fall back onto the sofas.

A loud gasp rose behind him accompanied by a huge crash of pottery and metal.

Morric partially turned to find Xavier staring at him. The tray filled with tea things strewn about his feet. Recently boiled water steaming around his bare feet.

"Xavier, the water—" Morric said. *An actual gasp from a dragon. This was bad.*

"A dragon has no fear of being scalded by water," Diarmid said.

Xavier learned against the nearest wall and dragged a hand through his hair. "What have I done?"

"There is no need for panic. We will figure out what all this means," Caderyn said.

"Caderyn, it's the mark—" Xavier shook his head. "I didn't believe the legends. It's been centuries. Eons."

Caderyn placed a hand on Xavier's shoulder to comfort the dragon. "Relax, my friend, it is good you called for us."

"Xavier?" Morric looked between Xavier and the Fae. "What is happening? No more secrets. Not about this. What does this dragon mean?"

"Before we get into the explanations, I wish to make sure this image is what we believe it is," Diarmid said. "May I first study your back?"

Morric moved until he stood in front of the taller Fae. He kept his eyes upon Xavier, those brilliant emerald eyes wide within a pale face. The shock literally covered Xavier's face and expression.

A light brush of warmth covered Morric's back while Diarmid used his healing abilities to scan him. As promised, the Fae didn't intrude any further than required. The Fae magic felt a bit different from his own, but there were similarities.

"The image remains true. No ink or scarring," Diarmid said. "The connection is there."

"How did it appear?" Morric asked.

"There isn't much history about these connection images. I understand it's a combination of the magical energy altering the pigmentation within the skin cells. How long were you asleep?"

"Two moons and this morning," Xavier said.

"Sounds about right for the magic to work through another gifted mate."

"Mate? Wait. What?" Morric looked between them.

"Xavier, perhaps you should take over the explanations," Diarmid said.

"I didn't know the legends were true and this could even happen. I've listened to the stories, but never believed..." Xavier trailed off and shook his head.

"Take it one step at a time," Caderyn said. "Other than the image upon his back, there's nothing wrong with Morric's health or magic. The image and the connecting magic are the explanation for the long sleep. Am I correct in this assessment of the situation, Diarmid?"

"That would be my understanding," Diarmid said. He held out the robe to Morric. "You can put this back on."

"Thank you," Morric said and covered himself. "Could I request a favor, Prince Caderyn?"

Caderyn tilted his head and nodded.

"If this other McShayne witch appears, could you alert Xavier to his presence? I would like to meet this other witch. Since I lost my family, I thought I was the last of my bloodline," Morric said.

"I'll let Xavier know. Xavier, do you need anything else?" Caderyn said.

Xavier walked over to Morric, glanced down at him.

Morric stared back, unable to figure out what was happening within the dragon.

"Morric was taken away from his beloved cabin and forest. The one against that evil small town that sends me the sacrifices," Xavier said.

"Aye, the forest is strong and healthy. I know the place."

"Could you find a way to protect it? Enchant it in a way to protect the cabin and forest, to forbid the townspeople go near it or destroy it. Or. I doubt this is beyond even the Fae's capabilities—"

"Go ahead and ask."

"Find a way to move it closer to the mountain. Perhaps you could create a special connection or passage for Morric to travel. If he returns without this enchantment or protection, I fear the town will discover him and kill him." Xavier caressed his fingers down Morric's cheek. "If this happens, my heart and soul will die with him."

"Xavier—" Morric said.

"This goes to the explanation about the meaning behind the image upon your back. If I lose my heart and soul, nothing but a mindless dragon is left behind," Xavier said.

"Which means?" Morric looked to the Fae.

"He would become a full dragon with no human inside him. While he could remain within the cave, there is the chance he would plunder and destroy to gather a horde or worse. If this happened, the dragon would need to be destroyed," Caderyn said.

"No. This can't be!" Morric gripped Xavier's forearms with his hands. "Xavier, you can't allow this to happen."

"It's already done," Xavier said.

"What? No." Morric shook his head.

"Explain the image, the connection to him. Now," Diarmid said.

Pulling in a deep breath, Xavier lowered his head. He lifted his gaze to find Morric. His eyes shone bright and true. "The dragon image upon your back was, what I believed, a myth among dragons."

Morric held still and let Xavier work out what he needed to tell him.

"Only a true heart mate could pass my natural defense, resist a dragon's seduction, and harm me. This happens to create balance within a relationship. When a dragon finds their heart mate, during an embrace they will emit blue flames and pure white smoke. Pure instinct drives this connection through the heart and blood."

Morric thought back to what happened in the hot springs. "The blue flames during the kiss."

"That's the fire. It shocked me to see it surrounding us. A legend coming true."

"Why did the flame appear?"

"You managed to do all three, Morric, during our first meeting. Everything that happened between us from the moment you woke to the second your lightning ball hit my chest—"

Morric touched Xavier's chest where the ball struck. "There was a mark. Damage."

"You were the first to mark me. First ever in my lifetime. This proves how each one of those pieces signaled how you, my gorgeous McShayne witch, are my mate."

"Your mate?"

"The proof of this connection is my dragon upon your back."

"And the runes curling around the tail?"

"Our names in dragon language. The syllables are unpronounceable in this form."

"This mingling of our blood and magic caused me to sleep so long."

"Like Diarmid thought, I believe that's what happened," Xavier said with a glance to the healer. "True heart mates are rare. Even more rare to find a mate in a witch. You have your own magic. Perhaps it caused an initial block and the magic needed to weave a way through in order to properly join the two without causing you harm."

"Witch and dragon united. By blood and magic. In me." Morric pressed his hand against his chest.

"A mating. An eternal match, Morric."

"Eternal?"

"Your lifetime will follow mine. I'm barely middle age for a dragon."

"Will I age?"

"I don't know. I believe the aging process slows, but again..."

"This connection is rare."

Xavier nodded when Morric finished the sentence.

Morric stepped back and dropped to the sofa. Everything would change in his life. It already changed the moment he woke chained to the post.

"Morric?"

"I can't remain within a mountain. My magic, my connection is to the forest, the land, Xavier. I don't have the same correlation with stone. It's actually my weakest link to all the elements."

"Ahh, now I understand what your request to me meant," Caderyn said while he crossed the room.

Xavier dropped to one knee and braced Morric's face between his hands. "I promise. I'll do everything I can with Caderyn and the Fae to figure this out. The decision to remain here with me is yours. It will always be yours with no pressure from me."

Tears dripped from Morric's eyes. He glanced to Caderyn. "Could you do what Xavier requests?"

"We can place wards around the cabin and forest. I'll make sure it's finished immediately to protect everything from the town. It'll give us time to figure out a way to connect you to the forest," Caderyn said.

"Is it possible?" Xavier asked. He stood to face Caderyn.

"I believe there is a way, but I must do some research," Caderyn said. "Give me a couple of moons. I must first stand within your forest to let my magic knit with it and then I'll create a portal to the entrance cavern. Xavier can activate it when you need to visit the forest and your cabin. Portals are limited and requires regeneration to maintain the link. They're useful until we discover something more permanent. Will this suit your needs?"

Morric glanced at Xavier, nodded, and returned to study Caderyn. "Yes. Aye. The town can't see or enter my lands?"

"The wards will send them off in different directions, never finding what they seek. It's how we keep pieces of the Fae realm from the mundane world," Caderyn said. "We'll let you continue your conversation. It's far more personal and Diarmid and I don't need to be here. We know our way out, Xavier. I'll contact you when I can connect the portal."

"Thank you, Prince Caderyn and Healer Diarmid," Morric said while he stood again to face them.

"It's a pleasure to meet you, Morric McShayne. If I see the other McShayne witch, I'll let both of you know."

Diarmid stepped closer. "This is a good match. Balanced. Let the love grow and blossom. The seeds are there within your hearts. Dragon, you have done well to find this witch. He'll keep you connected to reality."

"Thank you, Diarmid," Xavier said. "Thank you both for responding to my request for your assistance."

"You're family." Diarmid smiled at Morric. "Both of you are family. Anytime you need us. We'll be there."

Caderyn spoke his farewell offerings and left the cavern with Diarmid.

Chapter Seven

After the Fae left, Morric dropped back down on the sofa. Xavier moved to gather up the mess he created.

"Guess we never did end up having that cup of tea," Morric said. He picked up the small bag Diarmid left behind and twirled it between his fingers.

"I can make another pot."

"No, I can make a cup of it later." Morric tossed the bag on the low table to keep track of it. "There was a lot happening around here."

Xavier glanced over at him. "The last few days have been a bit overwhelming."

"That's putting it mildly." Morric lifted a hand and wiggled his fingers while he listed the crazy stuff. "Sacrifice. Dragon. Fae. Mate. Another McShayne." He shoved his fingers through his hair and fell back against the cushions.

"Nothing you would expect to ever happen."

"Not according to how my life went along, following the seasons and moons. My forest and cabin were all I needed."

Xavier looked away at Morric's words. He finished picking up the shattered porcelain and pottery to place on the tray. "Oh, to hellfire with this." With a wave of his hand, the entire mess including the spilled water vanished.

"A touch of magic is always helpful."

Xavier shrugged.

"Xavier, I..." Morric trailed off. "Please sit with me."

Xavier remained where he was. "Once Caderyn can create the wards around your home, I'll carry you there."

Morric sat forward. This wasn't what he expected to hear from Xavier. "What?"

"Soon as it's safe for you, you can go home. It's what you want."

"It was, aye, but the situation changed." Morric pointed a hand behind his back. "There is the matter of having a huge dragon appear upon my back. Something within us is connected."

"Not quite yet."

"Is there another step to finish the connection?"

"Aye," Xavier said. "If the last step isn't taken then the dragon will disappear from your body, but the link to me will always remain within you. Quiet and subdued within you. It's a form of protection from other dragons. It doesn't matter because you can return to your cabin and life. Which is what you desire."

"What about you?"

"I'll remain in my mountain. This is my territory and home. I have no desire to leave, but there's no reason for our paths to cross."

Morric realized what Xavier was trying to accomplish. Though he tried to do this in a rather odd fashion. Xavier wanted Morric to return to his life before the townspeople shackled him to the post. He wanted to give Morric everything he had asked for before their kiss in the hot springs that altered everything.

"What if I don't want to return to the cabin? Destiny and Fate offered me another path for my life. I can maintain my forest's health through the equinox dances if the prince can connect me. The earth is a vital part of my magic and base. Without it, I'm floundering, my magic unstable, and I'm downright grouchy and grumbly."

The dragon remained quiet.

Morric grimaced when nothing lightened the mood again. The dragon became far too serious. He needed answers about this connection. "Xavier, I need to know about this mate connection. Before we make any decisions about our lives. Decisions we will make together."

"What do you wish to know?"

"This final step. What's involved with finishing the connection?"

"Another exchange of my magic with words and promises. You drink some of my blood to combine our essence. The blue fire appears to seal the connection."

"Is this something like a handfasting?"

"Close to that."

"Is there a time limit?"

"Within a full moon cycle. I believe this is to make sure the couple understands what is happening and get to know each other." Xavier shrugged. "Again, this only comes from what I read within the legends. I never witness this type of mating."

"How do you know what to do?"

"There are books in my library filled with the legends and myths."

"There's a library around here. Why didn't you show me?"

Xavier's eyebrow winged up at the odd question.

"Sorry. I love books. Stupid question."

Xavier let out a quiet chuckle.

At least that seem to relieve some of the tension within him, Morric thought. "Dragons don't normally choose a mate."

"Not among other dragons. Other than a female with her brood, dragons remain solitary creatures. They come together for gatherings when females are ready to breed. It lasts a couple of moons and everyone returns to their territories. A female hatches and raises her brood, teaches them what they need to know, and will send them on their way when its time. Younglings, once leaving the nest, stay together another century for security reasons. As they age, they spread out to claim a territory."

"Do dragons mate with humans or Otherkin?"

"While we may be solitary, we do enjoy the comfort and attention of a lover. Many dragons have taken a mortal or Otherkin as their mate, but none were a true heart mate. None of them had the image of their mate's dragon etched upon their back."

"Is there anything else?"

"I suspect the same as any other mating, including making love with your mate."

"Everything to strengthen a connection, a bond, with another being."

"This is correct. A heart mate can be for eternity, the lifespan of a dragon." Xavier took hold of Morric's hand and kissed his fingers. "The decision remains yours. I'll accept your answer."

Morric twisted his hand to capture Xavier's hand. "What happens to the sacrifices?"

"What?"

Meeting Xavier's gaze, Morric kept his gaze steady. "I've been curious since our first meeting. What happened to the previous sacrifices?"

"They stay within the mountain for a couple of moons. To keep up the pretense, the dragon dropped them near a new town. I spread them over the course of multiple towns. When I leave them, they have clean clothes and a knapsack filled with clothing, food, water, supplies, and some gold. It wasn't their fault they ended up in this situation. I wanted to help give them a fresh start," Xavier said.

"Do any of them ask to stay?"

"A couple tried, but I kept none of them." Xavier held up his other hand. "If you accept the mating, all future sacrifices will be taken straight to a chamber for the designated time. Then taken to a town to begin a new life."

"No more seducing the sacrifices?"

"Once a dragon connects with a true heart mate, no one else will satisfy them. There's part of the legend, a true heart mated dragon can't even feel arousal or attraction to anyone else. A dragon is truly a loyal mate that'll never cheat."

"What happens if I don't accept the mating?"

"The situation with the sacrifices will be the same whether or not you accept." Xavier shifted to kneel on the floor in front of Morric. He took Morric's hands in his gentle grip. "I want to offer my love and life. Mate with me, be my partner. Exchange the words, the promises, and accept the blood of a dragon to join our lives. Help light the blue fire to finalize our connection. For as long as I live, you'll be by my side. As I age, you age."

"Other than a kiss and this dragon upon my back, we barely know each other. This is insane."

"Fate of a heart mate is never wrong. Fate matches a dragon with their true spirit and perfect connection. Plus, I recognized your spirit, courage, and magic." Xavier lifted Morric's hands and kissed his wrists and palms. He released one hand and tapped Morric's chest where his heart thumped. "I know your heart. According to the legends, it's a gift of all dragons when they meet their heart mate. Now I understand everything I read. Everything the legends spoke has come true for me. With my dragon upon your back, I know you're mine, Morric."

Xavier cupped Morric's face. He laid his lips gently upon his. The tender caress of their mouths set Morric aflame. That gentle touch sent a shockwave through his entire body.

Left breathless by the action, Morric licked his lower lip. "Not here. In your bed. Your chamber."

With a flash of magic, Xavier swept them back to his chambers. Their clothing disappeared and they nestled among the blankets.

"That's a handy trick," Morric said.

"It's useful," Xavier said. He turned to bring them to their knees, facing one another, and lifted their hands. "Repeat these words after me. You will naturally speak my language and understand the words with my magic."

The human roundness of his pupils altered to a dragon's slits while the irises became brilliant emerald flecked with gold. The powerful black wings appeared upon his back, spread out full and curled around them.

Soft lyrical syllables left Xavier's mouth. Morric understood every word and the meaning behind them.

Flickers of blue flames ignited around them.

The dragon and runes upon his back heated with the exchanged promises and blue flames.

Xavier released one hand and held up a finger. His finger altered to a dragon claw that he used to slice above his collarbone to access his heart blood. In the same lyrical language, he invited Morric to drink and unite them.

Morric leaned forward and licked the wound multiple times to take in the fiery blood. He could almost feel the blood move through him like liquid flames.

More words left while the flames rose higher and enclosed them within a fiery globe. A bolt of flame entered Xavier's back, flowed through him, and entered Morric's front. It exited his back and receded with the rest of the fire.

They collapsed together upon the blankets. Xavier's wings retreated into him. A light sweat covered their bodies, their cocks painfully swollen and erect.

Morric rolled Xavier to his back, captured his mouth with a savage intensity. He straddled Xavier's hips and ground down against him. He snagged Xavier's hands and held them over his head while he ground and rocked their bodies together.

With a show of strength, Xavier rolled them to Morric's back and leaned up. He used his teeth while his mouth ravaged Morric's. He moved down Morric's body and took Morric's cock in his mouth for a hard suck.

"Xavier!" Morric cried out while Xavier churned the energy within him toward that erotic edge. He opened his legs and pulled his knees back.

Xavier released his cock with a pop and continued to nibble and lick him everywhere.

Morric wrapped his legs around Xavier's shoulders to hold him tight against his body. He cried out when Xavier slid two slicked fingers deep inside him. He rocked hard against the hand now driving him mad.

"Inside me."

"Not yet. Give me more," Xavier said before he sucked on Morric's cock. He twisted, spread and used his fingers deep inside Morric.

When he found and relentlessly tapped that magical gland, Morric tumbled over the edge. He came hard, but his balls didn't release. He cried out. His legs tightened hard around Xavier's chest. He rocked and pulled away from those questing, maddening fingers that shot him over again. Again, his balls didn't empty. Frustrated and burning with need, Morric dug and dragged his nails against Xavier's shoulders.

"Enough. Enough. Inside. Fill me!" Morric demanded between breaths that burned. He tiptoed the edge, knowing he could easily tumble over again. "How... No..."

"Gift of a dragon while mating," Xavier said before his lips captured Morric's mouth.

Morric could taste himself within Xavier's flavor. He whined into the kiss when those fingers worked him, dragging around the sensitive opening.

Lifting back, Xavier called a bottle filled with golden liquid into his hand. He flicked open the corked top with his thumb and poured drops between them.

Those droplets felt like molten fire when those fingers slicked it inside him. Morric never encountered anything like this liquid.

"Dragon's oil. Special blend. Enhanced sensations and healing properties," Xavier said, but Morric barely understood.

Lost in ecstasy and desperation, Morric dug his fingers into Xavier's skin, whatever he could reach. His nails scraped and bit into the firm skin.

Xavier poured oil onto his hard cock. He corked and set the bottle aside. Then he grasped his cock and spread the oil. He thrust into his fist.

Morric rocked and shifted against those fingers buried in his ass. He lifted one leg higher around Xavier to drag him closer. "Now. Sweet Maiden, now!"

"Once more. Let me watch you fly." Xavier met Morric's passion clouded gaze. Then he gave the firm order. "Fly!"

Morric screamed with the next release. His back bowed off the mattress. That delicious oil and those fingers drove him tumbling over the fiery edge. He never felt those fingers leave him or the bite of pain when Xavier pushed his thick cock deep inside to the hilt.

Full. So full. Xavier filled him completely, stretched him almost to burning, but the oil glistened and slicked the way.

Morric dug his fingers into the blankets, finding something to hold onto while Xavier plunged harder and deeper. Each stroke varied in strength, speed and distance to enflame him. Every time, Xavier made sure to hit that blasted gland.

Morric's erect cock stood straight, engorged with need. It curled and bumped between their bellies. When Xavier grasped his cock with those oil slickened fingers, he screamed in need at the enhanced sensation. He thrust up into Xavier's tightening fist and down to meet Xavier's hard driving cock.

Covered in heat, filled with glory and fire, his hunger for the final climb sharpened and drove him to match Xavier's movements. Sweat covered Morric's body. Blood rushed through him, his skin flushed.

Xavier pulled out to the tip, playing with the sensitive ring. Morric keened high with a whimpering need. He plunged deep into him. Hard, fast and whipped them up to the highest peak.

Their gazes met. Their lips crushed together.

One final plunge and the world dropped. Their bodies shattered.

Searing ecstasy flooded Morric with uncontrollable joy. His lips quivered as gusts of desire rushed through him. Bolts of lightning jolted his body. Morric clamped like a vise around Xavier's cock and body.

When Xavier poured deep inside him with fiery seed, Morric spilled his release between their bellies. Flickers of continued energy rolled through them with aftershocks. Not letting up.

When the need released them, they sprawled across the blankets. Covered in oil, sticky seed, and sweat. Neither could find their breath.

"In the name of the Crone, I can't survive more of that," Morric muttered.

Xavier chuckled while he slipped free of Morric's body. He lifted his head from Morric's chest, his gaze a bit wicked and sleepy from shattered passion. "The Fates made us to fit together so our bodies soar. Oh, I believe we can do it again."

"Give me a few to find my breath. Next time. Your turn."

"Look forward to see what you got."

"First. Need to find my toes. Think I lost them after that second tumble," Morric said while he tried move.

"Could use a bit of help to find mine."

Soft laughter escaped, but Morric hissed when he stretched his limbs and rolled to the side.

Xavier cleaned them with magic.

"Definitely handy," Morric murmured.

Xavier spooned Morric, pressing his heart against the dragon splayed across Morric's back. His wings returned and tucked around them. While they tumbled into sleep, Xavier whispered, "Dragon's witch, my sacrifice and Fate's gift."

TO BE CONTINUED...

McShayne's Fae

About the Author

Dreamy...Sensual...Forever Love

A quiet one, Nicole Dennis is the penname of an asexual author of different genres of fiction – both LGBT+ and hetero. Lots of characters, worlds, and stories build up in her head until she must get them down on the screen – anything from romance to fantasy to paranormal.

During the day, she works in a quiet office in Central Florida, where she makes her home, and enjoys the down time to slip into her imagination. She is owned by a feline companion – a fluffy house panther, known as Midnight the Void. A very special furbaby who is FIV+ and polydactyl on her front paws (fluffy danger mittens!).

Contact & Media Info:

Website: http://nicoledennis.net

Email: nicoledennis.author@gmail.com

Facebook:

Main: www.facebook.com/NicoleDennis.Author

Page: https://www.facebook.com/NicoleDennis.Musings/

Group: https://www.facebook.com/groups/nicoledennis.author/

Amazon: https://www.amazon.com/author/nicoledennis

Threads: https://www.threads.net/@ndennis_author

Mastodon: https://mastodon.lol/@nicoledennis

QueeRomance: https://www.queeromanceink.com/mbm-book-author/nicole-dennis/

Goodreads: http://www.goodreads.com/author/show/2791975.Nicole_Dennis

CURRENT BOOKS:

Entwined Publishing/Pride Publishing

Southern Charm Series

1 – Rules of the Chef

2 – By the Numbers

3 – On the Green

4 – When in Bloom

5 – Following the Law

6 – According to Design

7 – Unexpected in the End (Coming 2025)

Freebies available on my website or email for PDF

Mischief Corner Books:

Secrets & Silk

Siren Publishing: (BookStrand.com)

Grant's Mechanic (MM)

Unholy Angel (MF Erotic Paranormal)

Fire Jaguars (MMF Paranormal)

1 – Fire Moon Dance

2 – Luna Moon Dance

3 – Dark Moon Dance

Other books are in the works

FatCat Books Ink (Self-Pub home):

New Stories:

Lyon Lynx Clan

Paws in the Snow (Prequel)

McShayne Bloodline

1 – McShayne's Dragon
2 – McShayne's Fae
3 – McShayne's Elf
4 – McShayne's Merman (Coming 2025)

Cheimon Tales

1 – Cracks in the Ice
2 – Strike's Stand (In the works)
3 – Mistletoe's Story (In the works)

Carnival of Mysteries (Multi-Author Collection)

1 – Dryad on Fire
2 – Flames of the Arcane

Re-Releases:
Walk Me Trilogy

1 – Walk Me Down the Middle
2 – Walk Me Through the Haze
3 – Walk Me Through the Darkness

7 Days of Christmas
Built Piece by Piece
At the Masquerade